Little Croc's Purse

For Jany, Phil, Ella, and Dom . . . who know how Little Croc felt!

Text and illustrations © 2010 Lizzie Finlay

First published in 2010 in Great Britain by Red Fox, an imprint of Random House Children's Books

This edition published 2011 in the United States of America by Eerdmans Books for Young Readers

an imprint of Wm. B. Eerdmans Publishing Co., 2140 Oak Industrial Dr. NE, Grand Rapids, Michigan 49505 / P.O. Box 163 Cambridge CB3 9PU U.K.

www.eerdmans.com/youngreaders

Manufactured at Tien Wah Press in Singapore, October 2010, first printing

10 11 12 13 14 15 16 17   9 8 7 6 5 4 3 2 1

ISBN 978-0-8028-5392-9   A catalog record of this book is available from the Library of Congress.

Jonelle Duracolour Loretta fabric design produced by Cavendish Textiles with acknowledgment to the John Lewis Partnership archive collection.

Little Croc's
Purse

Lizzie Finlay

. . . 51   52   53   54   55   56   57

Eerdmans Books for Young Readers
Grand Rapids, Michigan • Cambridge, U.K.

One lucky morning, Little Croc was playing hide-and-seek when he spotted something curious lying on the path.

It looked important . . . and valuable.

It smelled of *perfume*.

Excited crocodiles scurried from their hiding places.

"Wow! What is it?"
yelled Maddox.

"Where did you find that?"
squealed Sherlock.

"Open it!" shrieked Cedric.

Slowly, Little Croc untwisted
the clasps and tipped out the
heavy contents.

Out tumbled

five silver coins, seven golden coins, and a crisp 20-croc bill.

Everyone gasped.

Nobody noticed the secret something still hidden in the lining.

"**Wooooooooooooo-hoo!**" whistled Cedric.

"We're **rich**!"

"We could go **swimming!**" yelled Sherbet.

"Let's get some *lemonade*," shouted Oscar thirstily.

"Let's divide it quick," Monty insisted.
"**NO!**" said Little Croc. "I'm going to find the owner."

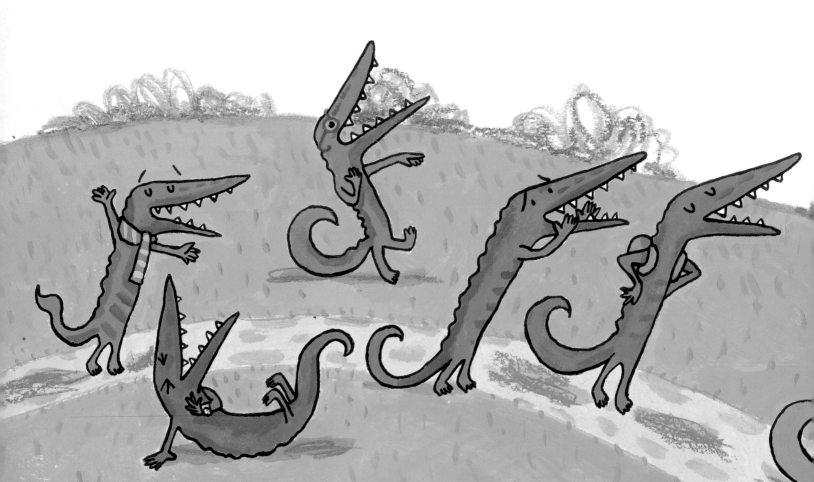

"No one returns things nowadays!"
the crotchety crocodiles called.
"Finders keepers," squawked Cedric.
"It's a waste of time and energy . . . **and money!**"
they cackled, cracking up laughing.
Little Croc ignored them and set off for the police station.

On the corner, Little Croc met a charity collector.
"Spare a few coins for a good cause?" he called.

"Sorry, sir," said Little Croc, "this isn't my money.
I'm searching for this lost purse's owner."

SHOE BY DOO

SALE
ONLY 15
CROCS

OPEN

In the window of his *favorite* shop, Little Croc gazed longingly at the boots. Would the owner notice if he borrowed some money from the purse?
"Yes! That'd be stealing," he said.

The purse was heavy and Little Croc was **VERY** thirsty.
"Surely the owner wouldn't mind if I bought
an ice-cold *lemonade* . . ." he sighed.
Suddenly, a terrible thought crept into his head.
"What if I kept the purse?"

"**NO!**" he scolded himself and
kept going toward the police station.
But around the next corner, he stumbled straight into . . .

... **Murdock!**

"My, what a **big** purse you've got!"

"I'm returning it to the owner," squeaked Little Croc.

"I lost my purse this morning," lied Murdock.

"How marvelous that you've found it!"

Little Croc felt trapped. "Come inside
with me and claim it?" he asked.

"Silly me," said Murdock, "my purse isn't pink . . .
But I am SO hungry. Lend me a few coins for
some chocolate cake?"

"Sorry, it isn't my money to spend. Good day, Murdock,"
said Little Croc, scrambling up the police station steps.

"Excuse me," Little Croc wheezed.

"I'm handing in this lost purse."

The police officer made a phone call. "It seems the owner, Mrs. Doolally, wants to meet you. She'll be here shortly."

Little Croc held his breath. "What will she be like?" he wondered.

Mrs. Doolally bustled in. "Honest crocs are so rare these days!" she said, inspecting the purse anxiously.

"Oh, thank goodness!" she cried, pulling out a beautiful locket from the secret inside pocket and opening it.

"That's my dear long-lost Claude . . . It's all I have to remember him by!" Mrs. Doolally hugged Little Croc tightly. "To thank you for your honesty, you can keep the purse."
Little Croc was gobsmacked.

Croc Monsieur's was the perfect place to celebrate.
"A freshly squeezed *lemonade*, three envelopes,
and a **pencil**, please," Little Croc ordered.
The lemonade tasted better than he'd ever imagined.

Little Croc divided his treasure into three envelopes labeled **spend**, **share**, and **save**.
He used his **spend** envelope to pay, and tucked the others safely into his purse. "Do you do deliveries?" he asked.

Little Croc rushed to his favorite shop and tried on his dream boots. *"Perfect!"* he squealed, paying for them out of his **spend** envelope.

"Thanks again, Mrs. D.," he whispered.

Then, Little Croc excitedly dropped three coins from his **share** envelope into the charity collector's jingling hat. "Bless you!" the man called after him. "Nice boots!"

At the toy store, Little Croc knew exactly what he wanted.

He paid the shopkeeper from the **share** envelope.

Little Croc found Murdock practicing
scary moves underneath the twisted tree.
It was embarrassing.

"I bought you a present," he said.

Murdock tore it open. Inside was a piggy bank.
It rattled. "I put some coins in to start you off,"
said Little Croc.

RICHTOWN   HOME

Murdock couldn't
stop smiling. It was
his first present ever.
Little Croc waved goodbye
and skipped off to find his friends.

"We knew you wouldn't find the owner!" the crocodiles jeered when they saw the floppy purse.

"I **FOUND** the owner," Little Croc said proudly.

"I **AM** the owner!" He grinned, showing all of his teeth. He couldn't help it.

"Mrs. Doolally gave the purse to me as a reward for being honest . . .

I bought myself these boots and a treat for **everyone!**"
he said, as the **Croc Monsieur's** delivery van arrived.
"**No Way!**" cried the crocs, rushing up to get
their lemonades.

That night, as Little Croc dropped his last coin into his piggy bank, a smile crept over his face.

If he could just save up enough, he'd seen a wonderful hat
to match his new boots . . .